MW00830007

THE MAYOR OF
CASTERBRIDGE

THE MAYOR OF CASTERBRIDGE

THOMAS HARDY

Om
KIDZ
An imprint of Om Books International

Reprinted in 2020

Om
KIDZ | **Om Books International**

Corporate & Editorial Office
A-12, Sector 64, Noida 201 301
Uttar Pradesh, India
Phone: +91 120 477 4100
Email: editorial@ombooks.com
Website: www.ombooksinternational.com

Sales Office
107, Ansari Road, Darya Ganj
New Delhi 110 002, India
Phone: +91 11 4000 9000
Fax: +91 11 2327 8091
Email: sales@ombooks.com

Adapted by Swayam Ganguly
Illustrated by Manish Singh, Manoj Kumar Prasad

ISBN: 978-93-85031-56-4

Printed in India

10 9 8 7 6 5 4 3 2

Contents

Chapter One

A Wife for Sale

It was a late summer evening. A young hay-trusser walked towards the large village of Weydon-Priors, in Upper Wessex. He was accompanied by his wife, who carried their child. The family was dressed simply but not in rags and the thick layer of dust that had gathered on their shoes and clothes bore testimony to a long journey. This led to an appearance that was impoverished and shabby.

The man boasted of an impressive figure; he was dark and looked rather strict. He was dressed in a short jacket of brown corduroy that appeared to be a recent purchase compared to

the rest of his suit, which consisted of a fustian waistcoat with white horn buttons, breeches, tanned leggings and a straw hat covered with black, glazed canvas.

He carried a rush basket on his back, secured by a loop strap. The crutch of a hay knife jutted out from one end of this basket and a wimble for hay-bonds was also visible.

His precise stride was the sluggish walk of the skilled countryman that varied from the purposeless, lazy walk of the general labourer. Each step and turn that he took showed a stubborn indifference towards everything.

What was really strange about this couple's appearance, and that could draw the attention of any passerby who would otherwise have overlooked them, was the fact that they did not exchange a single word as they walked.

The man was reading, or pretending to read, a ballad sheet which he held with some difficulty in a hand that protruded from under the basket strap. But he didn't speak with the woman and neither did she think about taking his arm companionably even once, as they walked side by side. The man never thought about offering it to her and it appeared that the lack of spoken words between the two was natural and of mutual acceptance. The only words that could be heard were the soft, rare murmurs of the mother to the infant cradled in her arms — who babbled in reply.

The only time the young woman's face appeared attractive was when she glanced at her baby. The rays of the sun caught her face and made her look almost beautiful. She trudged on, lost in thought. It was obvious to any observer that the couple were husband and wife and the parents of the little girl. It was the only relationship that seemed possible, considering the air of wilted familiarity that the three shared, while they walked together like a raincloud down the road.

The surroundings were silent except for the stray sound of a bird weakly breaking into an evening song. But as they neared the village, they were greeted by shouts and other noises that emerged from a distant elevated spot camouflaged by the trees. When they finally sighted the houses that outlined Weydon-Priors, they came across a turnip hoer carrying a hoe on his shoulder, from which his dinner bag hung.

"Any trade happening here?" the man asked the turnip hoer, pointing in the direction of the village.

"Anything in the hay-trussing line?" the man enquired again, thinking his question hadn't been comprehended.

The turnip hoer replied in the negative.

"Is there a small cottage or a newly built house to let?" the man enquired.

"Weydon believes more in pulling down rather than building," the man replied pessimistically. "Why, as many as five houses were cleared away last year and three this year."

The man, who was a hay-trusser, asked the turnip hoer if anything was going on in the

village and was told that it was the Fair Day celebrations, although it was to end that day.

The hay-trusser and his family walked on to enter the Fairfield where standing places and pens stood. Hundreds of sheep and horses were being displayed and sold. Most of them had been taken away and the pens stood almost empty, barring the inferior animals that were up for sale. Despite this, the crowd was thicker now as compared to the one in the morning, which included a lot of classy traders. The party included merry visitors, like holidaying journeymen, a few soldiers and village shopkeepers with entertainment in the form of peep-shows, toy-stands, waxworks, created monsters, quacks, thimble-riggers, vendors selling knick-knacks and soothsayers.

The family looked around for a tent serving refreshments and spotted two suitable tents that were equidistant. 'Good Home-brewed Beer, Ale and Cyder' the first one announced and

the placard of the second proclaimed, 'Good Furmity Sold Hear'.

The man chose the first tent, but the woman wanted to visit the second one because she liked furmity, which was refreshing after a long day. The man gave in to her protestations and they entered the second tent.

A large crowd was gathered inside, seated at the long, narrow tables laid inside the tent on either side. A stove with a charcoal fire rested at the upper end and a big three-legged crock made of bell-metal hung overhead. A woman, who looked 50 years old, slowly stirred the pot and prevented the strange mixture of corn in the grain, milk, flour, raisins, currants and other things, from burning. The man and his wife ordered a bowl each of the concoction and sat down to eat.

But there was more for the patrons in this tent than what met the eye.

The man had been following the hag's movements from the corner of his eye and winked at her, passing up his basin after she nodded. She produced a bottle from under the table and measured out a miserly quantity, to pour it into the man's bowl. It was rum. The man was equally sly in paying her. The concoction was strong enough for the man's taste. The wife, who had been watching this transaction, looked at him with some concern, but the man persuaded her to have her drink laced with a much smaller quantity of liquor.

The man finished the drink and ordered a stronger portion. He proceeded to have a third and a fourth and his mood changed from serene to jovial, and then meddlesome as he was finished with his drinks. He started arguing for no reason and was extremely bitter about his circumstances.

"I was a fool to have married at 18," he complained. "My situation now is the result of that mistake. Though I am a skilled and experienced hand in my line, I have only 15 shillings with me."

And then the man heard the cries of the auctioneer who was selling old horses in the field outside.

"I don't see why men cannot sell off their unwanted wives just like gypsies sell their old horses," the man said, suddenly. "Why, I'd sell my wife in a jiffy if anyone would buy her!"

"Michael, this is not the first time you have uttered nonsense in public. You have said this too many times," she warned her husband.

"I know I've said it before, but I mean it," he replied.

Then, "Is there anyone who will buy her?" he suddenly asked the gathering, loudly. "Stand up and show yourself, Susan," he ordered his wife, who meekly obeyed.

"Five shillings," someone said and everyone laughed aloud.

"Five guineas or nothing," the husband said. "For the last time, do I have a buyer?"

"Yes!" a voice boomed from the doorway and everyone turned to see a sailor at the door.

He had entered just a while ago. The sailor threw five banknotes on the table which added up to five pounds.

"I do this assuming that the young woman agrees to this proposal. I do not want to hurt her feelings," the sailor stated.

"She is willing only if the child accompanies her," her husband declared. "Do you swear to that?" the sailor asked Susan.

"I do," she replied.

"Come along," the sailor smiled and said to her, "The more, the merrier."

Susan caught hold of the sailor's arm with her right hand and clutched her daughter with her left. Sobbing, she walked out of the tent.

Chapter Two

Casterbridge

The man woke up the next morning and looked around the empty tent. He discovered his wife's ring on the floor and the events of the previous night returned in his memory. For a while, he was lost in thought.

"I must get her and little Elizabeth-Jane back from the sailor," he decided.

Carrying his rush basket, he left the tent and looked around. It was a fresh September morning and he spotted the village below. The sun had just come up and the gypsies and showmen were still asleep in their carts. So, none of them saw the hay-trusser leave Weydon

Fairfield, except a stray dog. After travelling for a mile, he reached a lane and stood near a gate.

'Did I reveal my name to anyone last night?' he thought, and then came to the conclusion that he hadn't.

He was surprised that his wife had agreed to this charade without a protest. He felt that she had been eager to participate in this event. 'Did she believe that this transaction was real?' He was sure of one thing: Susan lacked levity of character and possessed an intellect that was extreme in its simplicity. Maybe, there was a certain foolhardiness and wounded pride hidden beneath the layer of serenity that had made her ignore all doubts.

On previous occasions, when he had talked of selling her — the way he had done last night — she had told him resignedly, in a tone of passive acceptance, that she would not hear of it. "But she must know I am not in my senses when I make those statements," he mumbled.

He decided to keep walking and keep looking till he located his wife and daughter.

"How could she disgrace me so?" he ranted aloud to no one. "It is just like Susan to display such simplicity. Her meekness has done me the most damage than the foulest of tempers has done to men."

He calmed down soon and decided to find her and little Elizabeth-Jane at any cost.

'I must put up with this shame as best as I can,' he thought. 'It is my own doing.'

Then, he took an oath; an oath that was stronger than any he had ever taken before. But he decided to do so at the right place. After travelling for a while, he reached the premises of a church.

After resting his head on the clamped book, he said aloud, "I, Michael Henchard, take an oath before God on this morning of 16th September, I shall avoid all strong liquors for 21 years, beginning today, to mark the 21 years

I have lived. May I be struck blind, deaf and dumb, if I break this oath!"

Henchard then began searching for his missing wife and child. He had no money and the shame over his actions prevented him from conducting a thorough search. So, he received no clue about his family's whereabouts.

Days turned to weeks, then stretched to months. And one day, he arrived at a seaport where he learnt that the people who matched the description had emigrated not long ago.

Henchard travelled in the south-west direction, the very next day till he reached the town of Casterbridge, located in a distant corner of Wessex.

Chapter Three

Deja Vu

Years later, two women walked hand-in-hand on the highroad into the village of Weydon-Priors. The first woman was none other than the wife of Henchard; older and dressed in the garb of a widow. Her companion was also dressed in black and was a presentable woman of 18. She was Susan Henchard's grown up daughter, Elizabeth-Jane. While time had hardened Susan Henchard's features, it had transferred her youthful qualities to her daughter. They reached the fair on the outskirts of the village. Now, there were some mechanical improvements that had been brought about by time in the

roundabouts and high-fliers. The machines for testing rustic strength and weight had seen noticeable improvements, but the real business of the fair had gone down drastically. The trade that had existed here for centuries had been adversely affected by the flourishing markets that now existed in the neighbouring towns. The sheep pens and the horses' tie-ropes had been halved and the stalls featuring traders, like tailors, hosiers, coopers and linen-drapers had almost been forced to quit.

"Why did we waste our time by coming here?" the daughter exclaimed.

"I had a reason, my dear Elizabeth," the mother replied. "I first met Newson here on a day like this."

"It's a pity that father is no more with us," Elizabeth-Jane replied, sadly. Her mother hesitated, and then continued, "This was the same place where I last saw the man we are looking for, Mr Michael Henchard."

"Is he a near relation?"

"No, he was a hay-trusser and he never knew you."

"I don't think it'll be helpful enquiring here for anyone," the daughter concluded.

"I can't be sure about that," the mother, who was now called Mrs Newson, replied. At the fair, she met the same woman in the tent who was now a bent, wrinkled old hag with no customers except two small boys.

"Do you remember," Susan whispered to the old hag, after ensuring that her daughter was standing at a stall which was far away, "the sale of a wife by a husband 18 years ago in your tent?"

"The only reason I remember that man," the old woman replied, "is because he returned to leave a message that if a woman should come looking for him, he could be found at Casterbridge."

"I have learnt what I wanted to," Susan told her daughter. "He is in Casterbridge which is a long way from here. But we shall go there."

The mother and daughter left the fair and went to the village to find a place to stay the night.

For so many years, Susan Henchard had not disclosed the true story of her life to her daughter. Elizabeth-Jane had grown up believing that Mr Newson was her father and that her parents shared a normal relationship.

After 'purchasing' Susan, Newson had taken Susan and Elizabeth-Jane to Canada, where they lived for many years without much material success. They had returned to England, when Elizabeth-Jane was 12, to settle in Falmouth. Newson had worked as a boatman and a general handy shoreman there, for a couple of years, before travelling for trade to Newfoundland.

It was during this time that Susan experienced an awakening. She had once confided in a friend about her past, who had mocked her for accepting Newson's proposal. When Susan had told him that she could not live with him anymore, Newson had become very unhappy.

A few months after Newson had left home on the Newfoundland trade again, news reached Susan that he had been lost at sea.

This solved Susan's dilemma. She had been troubled by her sense of morality. After reflecting for a considerable amount of time, she had decided to look for Henchard, who was her real husband.

On a Friday evening, in the middle of September, Susan and Elizabeth-Jane reached the peak of a hill about a mile away from Casterbridge. They sat down to rest and overheard two arguing men on the other side.

"Didn't those two men take the name of Henchard in their conversation?" Elizabeth-Jane asked her mother, after the two men left.

"Yes, he must still be at Casterbridge then," Susan replied, grimly.

The two women resumed their journey and reached an old church to hear the bell. This was a practice in Casterbridge and was the signal to shut all shops and end the day's business. They

asked a woman they met near the market where they could find a baker.

"There's more good beer in Casterbridge than good bread now," the woman replied.

"But why isn't there any good bread?" Susan asked.

"It is the corn factor, the man that all our bakers and millers deal with," the woman replied. "He sold them grown wheat and they didn't know it was grown. Now, the loaves are as flat as toads and hard inside."

Mother and daughter bought some biscuits at a shop and instinctively headed to a nearby place from where they could hear music. The building they reached was called the King's Arms, the most reputed hotel in Casterbridge.

"We must make enquiries about Mr Henchard here," Susan whispered to her daughter and urged her to do the needful. The girl singled out an old man.

"What's happening tonight?" she asked.

"It's a big public dinner of the gentlemen in town with the Mayor in the chair," he replied.

A man, who was about 40, sat in the special chair facing the window. He boasted of a bulky frame, large features and had a commanding voice. The hay-trusser was now the Mayor of Casterbridge.

"I have seen him and it is enough for me," Susan mumbled. "Now, I can die in peace."

"What?" Elizabeth-Jane asked her mother. "I thought he looked like a kind man. Don't you think he will befriend us?"

"I don't know, but I don't wish to see him again," her mother replied.

Elizabeth-Jane didn't persist. She noticed that though everybody in the gathering drank, the Mayor sipped only water and nobody filled his glass. Curious, she asked a man standing nearby about this anomaly. He told her that the Mayor did not touch drink liquor. "I've heard he took a gospel oath many years ago," the man confided in her. "He hasn't touched a drop of liquor since."

"How long does he have to suffer?" another man, who had overheard him, asked.

"Another two years," was the reply.

"Does he have many men?" Elizabeth-Jane asked.

"Many? Why, he is the most powerful member of the town council," the old man replied. "He's also an important man in the surrounding county and has big business dealings in wheat, oats, barley, hay and roots. Henchard's got his hands in everything. He worked up from nothing at all, when he arrived here, to eventually become the pillar of Casterbridge. But this bad corn business has shaken him up a little, recently."

The dinner had concluded and speeches were being made. Henchard's voice boomed over the rest.

"All that is very well," a voice from a gathering of minor tradesmen interrupted him. "But what about the bad bread?"

Michael Henchard's face darkened.

"You must keep in mind that the weather before the corn harvest was the worst in many years," he replied. "My business is too large for me to look after it alone, I have advertised for an expert to manage my corn department. I hope these mistakes won't happen once that person joins me."

"Will you replace the grown flour we have now with the good grain?" a miller demanded and Henchard's face darkened further. He drank from his water tumbler as if to calm down, or to gain time before his reply.

"If there's anybody here who can teach me how to turn grown wheat into wholesome wheat, I shall take it back gladly," he finally replied. "But we all know, it is an impossible feat. It can't be done!"

Chapter Four

The Mayor Meets the Expert

The group outside the window at the King's Arms had swelled up by now and a handsome young stranger with a pleasant disposition had joined it. When he heard the last words of Henchard's speech, he made a small note in his pocketbook with the help of the light by the window. He tore the paper, folded it and handed it to one of the waiters.

"Give this to the Mayor immediately," he instructed.

Elizabeth-Jane had been watching him and had been instantly attracted to the young man's mannerisms and Scottish accent.

"Can you let me know of a hotel that is respectable but priced more moderately?" the man from Scotland (he appeared to be from the northern part), asked the waiter.

"The Three Mariners, just below, is a good place," was the reply.

The stranger thanked him and headed out. His note reached Henchard, who read it slowly, and its content forced him into deep thought. The subject of wheat had been forgotten by now, the speeches had given way to songs.

The clock struck nine and Elizabeth-Jane suggested to her mother that they should look for lodgings at the inn called The Three Mariners. And the two left. The Mayor found an excuse to leave the chair and found out from the waiter that the stranger had left for The Three Mariners. He decided to go there at once.

Elizabeth-Jane and her mother were shown into a small room at the inn.

Elizabeth-Jane headed to the bar and offered the landlady her services as her mother was

tired. She helped the landlady serve the meals to the residents.

Soon, Elizabeth-Jane carried supper to the Scotsman's suite, realising it was right next to their own room. She left without speaking to him, but when she entered her room, she was surprised to see that her mother was still awake. Susan lifted her finger to her lips as her daughter entered. Elizabeth-Jane realised the room that had been allotted to them had once served as the dressing-room for the suite that the Scotsman's now occupied. So, one could hear whatever was spoken there.

"It is the Mayor," her mother whispered, and Elizabeth-Jane could hear their conversation.

"My name is Donald Farfrae and I'm in the corn trade," the young Scot was saying, "I'm going to Bristol from where I hope to wish to travel to other parts of the world to try my luck, especially in the great wheat-growing western districts. There is no scope here for developing my inventions to enhance this trade."

"I am sincerely grateful for the words you wrote to me," Henchard said. "I'd like you to prove them to me, but I'm sure I'll have to pay you before you reveal anything."

The young man said that he'd be more than willing to share his knowledge with Henchard and that he had a sample in his bag. Then, the young man unlocked his case and there was a technical discussion about how many ounces to the bushel, drying, refrigeration and so on. The young man gave him some grains to taste and Henchard was satisfied with the results.

"Although my business is in both corn and hay, I understand hay much better," Henchard confessed.

He then offered the young man the managerial position of the corn branch with a handsome salary, including a commission. But Farfrae refused, saying he had to leave the next day. He also refused to accept payment from Henchard for the trade secrets he had shared.

"I shall never forget this generosity," Henchard promised. "That too from a complete stranger," he wondered.

Farfrae offered Henchard a drink, but he refused.

"I was ruined by drink when I was a young man," Henchard declared as he rose to take his leave. "It made me do something I shall repent till my death. I vowed that very day not to touch liquor for as many years as my age was on that day. Although I have kept my oath, there are days when I'm so dry that I feel I can drink up a quarter-barrel. But my oath ensures I do not touch any kind of strong liquor."

After Henchard left, Donald Farfrae was tempted to join the lively crowd below and soon made some new friends among the tradesmen who were drinking at the hotel bar. Elizabeth-Jane was present too and she was mesmerised, just like the rest of the crowd, when Farfrae started singing.

When he sang sadly, Elizabeth-Jane felt a tear at the corner of her eye. None of them had heard anyone sing like this before and when Farfrae finished, he was greeted by thunderous applause followed by silence which was even more generous than the applause. But one song was not enough for the crowd, and the Scotsman was compelled to sing again. Henchard heard him sing through the heart-shaped holes fashioned in the window-shutters and stayed to listen.

"There is something really good about that man," Henchard confessed. "Or maybe, I feel this way because I'm a lonely man. I'd have given him one-third of my business had he decided to stay back."

Chapter Five

Henchard's Plan

Henchard met Farfrae as the latter was leaving the inn. Elizabeth-Jane overheard their conversation from the window of her room.

"My lad, you should have been a wise man and joined me," Henchard said.

"It might have been a wise move, but my plans are uncertain," Farfrae replied. The two men had left the inn's vicinity, and were now out of Elizabeth-Jane's hearing range.

'A good man is gone,' she thought sadly.

Suddenly, a procession of five huge wagons rolled in to stop under the window. The hay that was piled up in the wagons reached up to

the bedroom windows. A little board on each wagon said, in white lettering,

HENCHARD, Corn-Factor and Hay-Merchant.

Meanwhile, Susan was convinced that she should make a conscious effort to join Henchard for her daughter's sake. She decided to send Elizabeth-Jane with a message to him, which said that his relative Susan, a sailor's widow, was in town.

Susan had decided to get in touch with him because of two things: Henchard had been described as a lonely widower and he had been heard expressing his anguish over his past deeds. Elizabeth-Jane arrived at Henchard's house with the message, but he was not there, instead, she was guided to the store-house office of the estate.

To her surprise, she was met by Mr Farfrae there. Henchard had convinced Farfrae to join him. Henchard had been so desperate that he had asked Farfrae to name his own terms.

Farfrae told Elizabeth-Jane that Henchard was busy at the moment and he asked her to wait. Soon, Henchard arrived and he received Susan's message. He was very happy and he led his daughter, who was still unaware of Henchard's true relationship with her mother, to his home after a warm welcome. Elizabeth-Jane informed him how they had lost her father at sea and were now staying at The Three Mariners. Henchard then wrote a small note for her mother, put it in an envelope and added five pounds in it. As an afterthought, he also put five shillings in it, sealed the letter and handed it to Elizabeth-Jane for her mother. He had been so warm towards Elizabeth-Jane that the girl, not having had many friends, was almost moved to tears. Susan received the letter and opened it in isolation. It said,

Meet me at eight this evening at the Ring on the Budmouth Road. The girl appears to be unaware of our association. Keep it so till I have seen you.

M.H.

There was no mention of the five guineas he had enclosed in the letter, but Susan understood. She was excited about the meeting and couldn't wait for it to be evening. Though she had told Elizabeth-Jane that she had been invited by Mr Henchard to meet him, she did not disclose the details or reveal the contents of his note and her letter.

One of the finest Roman amphitheatres was called The Ring at Casterbridge and the architecture of ancient Rome was reflective in its every nook, corner and alley. Henchard had chosen this spot to meet Susan primarily because of the isolation it offered and also because it was easy to locate a stranger like her. The two met in the middle of the arena and neither spoke. Susan simply leaned against Henchard who held her in his arms.

"I don't drink now, Susan," he said, slowly. "I haven't had a sip since that night."

He paused for a while and continued, "If only I had known that you were still alive!

I had every reason to believe that both you and the child had perished. I tried to find you by all possible means but failed. Why were you silent for so long, Susan?" he demanded.

"O Michael! It was all for him and no other reason," Susan replied. "I thought I owed it to him to be faithful. I believed that the bargain was true and binding. I am meeting you now as his widow and with the thought that I have no claim upon you. I would have never met you had he not died."

"Well, we must devise a way now to keep Elizabeth-Jane in the dark and set matters straight," Henchard said, thoughtfully. "I have a plan. You and Elizabeth-Jane must take up a cottage in town. Then, I shall meet you as the widow Mrs Newson, court you and marry you. Elizabeth-Jane shall enter my house as a step-daughter and I shall have the good fortune of being reunited with my wife and daughter. This will be a secret between the two of us."

"The thought of being married to you again is an encouraging one," Susan replied. "After all that has happened in the past, it does seem to be the right course of action. I shall return to Elizabeth now and inform her that our kinsman, Mr Henchard wants us to stay on in town."

Chapter Six

Reunited

Henchard shared his story with Farfrae and told him how he had once lost his wife but had now got her back.

"But Farfrae," Henchard declared sadly, "by accepting Susan, I have wronged another innocent woman who is much younger than her."

Henchard explained, "During the potato and root season, I often had to go to Jersey on business. One autumn, I fell seriously ill while I was there and this young lady took pity on me. She took me into her home and nursed me back to health. She was from a good family and as lonely as I had been. Both of us planned to

marry soon. A scandal occurred because I was in her house and as soon as I was well, I returned. But she suffered a lot in society after I left, which I gathered from her letters. I intended to marry her, but now that Susan is back in my life, there is no way I can do so. My first duty is towards Susan and our child. However, I must send some money to the other lady. Can you help me in this regard?" he requested.

Farfrae agreed.

"Please write an explanation to her of whatever I have told you. I'm bad at writing letters. Please break it gently to her," Henchard said.

Farfrae carefully drafted the letter for Henchard. After he had left, Henchard copied the contents and put it in an envelope, enclosing a cheque in it. He went to the post-office and walked back after posting the letter.

'Can it all end so easily?' he thought worriedly. 'God knows! But I must make things right for Susan and Elizabeth-Jane now.'

Henchard hired a cottage for Susan in the upper part of town, near the Roman wall and its surrounding avenue under the name Mrs Newson, in accordance with their plan. As soon as the mother and daughter were settled in their new home with a servant, Henchard started visiting them for tea. The visits increased and soon they became the topic of gossip in Casterbridge.

The fact that the vain Mayor had been largely aloof from the company of women added fuel to the fire despite the fact that everybody was aware they were related in some manner. The boys in town had nicknamed Mrs Henchard 'The Ghost' on account of her paleness. Henchard determinedly set about to unify or rather reunify the relationship with this pale woman and soon, Susan Henchard entered a carriage for the first time in her life.

On her wedding day, a brougham took her and Elizabeth-Jane to church. As the November rain fell in a drizzle, Mr and Mrs Henchard

exchanged vows once again. Only Donald Farfrae, who was the groom's best man, was aware of the secret other than the couple. Elizabeth-Jane discovered that her life changed entirely when her mother married Mr Henchard. She had never encountered greater freedom, or had access to such wealth before. The easy and affluent life that she was ushered into after her mother's wedding thrilled her. She could now possess all the material possessions and ornaments she desired. With this new change and refinement came beauty but Elizabeth-Jane was not spoilt with the acquisition of sudden wealth and prosperity.

'I refuse to indulge in too much, come what may,' she promised herself. Elizabeth-Jane soon became a favourite of Henchard and she accompanied him on his visits more than she went out with her mother. One morning, as the three breakfasted, Henchard noticed that Elizabeth-Jane's hair colour was light brown.

"Didn't you tell me that Elizabeth-Jane's hair would be black when she was a baby?" he asked his wife suddenly, taking her completely by surprise.

"Did I?" Mrs Henchard mumbled after she had jerked his foot as a sign of warning. After Elizabeth-Jane had left for her room, Henchard apologised to his wife, "I completely forgot for a while. What I had meant was Elizabeth-Jane's hair looked as if it would be darker than it is now when she was little."

"Yes," Susan agreed. "But the colour of hair changes so much in a girl as she grows up."

"I was aware that their hair gets darker," Henchard replied. "But does it lighten as well?" he enquired.

"Oh, yes," his wife replied quickly.

"Susan, I insist that she be renamed Miss Henchard now instead of Miss Newson," Henchard stated firmly. "I shall advertise it in the Casterbridge paper and I'm sure she won't object to this."

But Elizabeth-Jane did object to this idea and preferred to be called Miss Newson, so Henchard had to abandon the idea. Meanwhile, Henchard's business was thriving under the competent supervision of Donald Farfrae and was reaching new heights. Letters and ledgers replaced the earlier system of Henchard conducting business, dependent on his memory and word of mouth transactions. Everything was now recorded and made systematic by Farfrae. Donald and Henchard were inseparable and Henchard thought of him as a younger brother.

One day, Elizabeth-Jane received an anonymous letter asking her to meet the writer at a granary on Durnover Hill. She went and waited. After a while, she saw Donald Farfrae approach. But he denied that he had written the note or that he had sent for her.

"That person is not likely to come," Farfrae concluded after a while. "Maybe someone has played a trick on you, which is a pity as we are

wasting our time here with so much work to be done."

Elizabeth-Jane praised his performance at The Three Mariners and he said that he would sing for her whenever she wanted.

"Do not mention about this hoax to anyone, Miss Newson," he said to her. "That's the only way to call the bluff of the person who wrote that note. But look, there's wheat husk and dust on your dress," he exclaimed.

"The only way to clean it is by blowing on it," Farfrae suggested and when Elizabeth-Jane did not object, Donald Farfrae began to blow air on her dress, her hair and her neck.

Chapter Seven

The Rift

At 6 pm, the last worker to leave was Abel Whittle. Poor Abel always overslept and as a result reported late for work. He seriously wished to be among the earliest workers to come for work. But his comrades always forgot to pull the string he attached to his toe and left hanging outside his window every night before he slept. Henchard had warned him about coming to work late but somehow, Whittle could never manage to do so. Henchard warned him for the last time that if Abel was late again, Henchard would personally come and drag him out of bed. But there was no sign of Abel

again the next morning. Henchard stormed off to Abel's house and shook the man awake.

"Off to work," he ordered. "Never mind your breeches!"

Abel unhappily put on his waistcoat and meekly followed Henchard. They met Farfrae on the way and Abel complained to him.

"Go home, put on your breeches and come to work like a man," Farfrae ordered him.

"Who is sending this man back home?" Henchard demanded.

"I am," Farfrae replied.

"Get up on that wagon, Whittle," Henchard ordered.

"He won't if I am the manager," Farfrae said. "Either he goes home and puts on those breeches, or I walk out of here never to return."

Henchard stared angrily at Farfrae, who refused to give in.

Henchard, who had once been the most respected man in his circle, soon found his popularity diminishing. Instead of him, people

now sought the opinion of Donald Farfrae. They thought he was cleverer, more approachable and knowledgeable, and possessed a better temper. Many of the workers secretly wished that Farfrae was the their master, instead of Henchard.

One day, Farfrae requested Henchard to lend him and his friends some rick-cloth. Preparations for a national event were underway. Farfrae and his associates wanted to put up a show at a nominal charge to entertain the residents of Casterbridge. Henchard agreed, but the devious Mayor planned to put up his own entertainment show free of charge to spoil Farfrae's party.

Henchard chose a spot close to town that was elevated and green. It sloped to the River Froom and offered a fine view of the surrounding countryside. Henchard advertised about the event extensively in large, pink posters and personally supervised the men when they set up the climbing poles offering cheese and smoked ham at the top. The best of entertainment and sports was planned with hurdles, boxing and wrestling stages. There were games to be held like wheelbarrow racing with donkeys, sack races and whoever could walk across the slippery pole laid across the river would win the pig tied at the other end. Henchard also ensured that a grand tea would be provided for everyone free of cost. But on the day of the celebrations, the sky opened up and it rained incessantly.

There was a fierce storm and Henchard realised, gloomily, that his grand project had died a natural death before it had even commenced. However, by six in the evening, the storm had abated and it looked like the fair could go on after all. But most people had already left to attend Farfrae's event in the West Walk by this time. Disgruntled, Henchard had to give orders to shut shop and he headed to West Walk to see how things were progressing there. He saw Farfrae clad in the traditional costume of a Highlander, standing amidst the dancers. He could see the genuine admiration in the women's faces as Farfrae danced. Henchard's wife and daughter were among the onlookers.

"The Mayor lacks the qualities that this young man possesses," he overheard a man saying. "Where would his business be without Farfrae?"

Henchard saw Farfrae dancing with Elizabeth-Jane. The quaint, little dance was soon over and Henchard's daughter quickly glanced at him for his approval. But she did not receive it.

"You should have held your sport event in such a sheltered place," a friend of Henchard's advised him, good-naturedly. "That's where you were beaten by him."

"He's going to beat you at your game soon and walk away with everything," Mr Tubber added in jest.

"No, he won't," Henchard replied. "Instead, he will leave me soon."

Elizabeth-Jane had gauged from Henchard's behaviour that she had made a mistake by dancing with Farfrae and this thought made

her miserable. She decided to go home.

"May I walk you home, Miss Newson?" Farfrae, who had followed her, asked. She agreed, and the two began walking.

"I shall leave you soon," Farfrae said.

"Why?" she asked.

"It's simply a matter of business and nothing else," Farfrae replied. "But it is for the best. Although I had hoped for an opportunity for another dance with you."

"I'm afraid I am not a good dancer like you," she said.

"But you are," Farfrae insisted. "But I'm afraid I have offended your father and I might have to leave this town."

Elizabeth-Jane sighed.

"I wish I was a richer man, Miss Newson and that your father was not offended with me. If it was so, I would have asked something of you tonight. But sadly, that is not meant for me," he said, and then changed the topic, "I have never discovered who sent us both to Durnover's

granary that day. Perhaps they wanted us to stay there and talk to each other. I do hope that you folks at Casterbridge won't forget me when I leave."

"Of course we won't," she said in an earnest manner. "In fact, I wish you would never leave."

The two then said goodbye and went their separate ways.

Chapter Eight

The Death of a Good Woman

Word soon spread around Casterbridge that Henchard and Farfrae had decided to go their separate ways. Elizabeth-Jane was anxious to know if Farfrae was leaving town, and was happy when she found out that he wasn't. In fact, he had bought the business of a man, who was in the same trade as Henchard, albeit on a smaller scale. Farfrae had decided to be a corn and hay merchant in Casterbridge.

Henchard ordered Elizabeth-Jane not to see Farfrae anymore and even wrote to him, forbidding him from meeting his daughter. Northern insight was up against Southern

doggedness. Farfrae and Henchard locked horns against each other as they engaged in a commercial war. The two men encountered each other every Saturday in the crowded marketplace, but while Donald Farfrae was always willing and eager to talk to Henchard, the Mayor avoided him like the plague. Now, even the name Donald Farfrae was forbidden from being mentioned in the Mayor's house.

Meanwhile, Mrs Henchard had been taken ill suddenly and Elizabeth-Jane was nursing her day and night. One morning, Henchard was eating breakfast by himself, and he received a letter from Jersey. The letter writer said that she realised that further communication between them was impossible now that he had re-married. She requested him to return all the letters he had received from her and all her things. She thanked him for the generous sum he had sent her and informed him that she was enroute to Bristol to meet a rich relative.

The letter said in conclusion:

I shall return via Casterbridge. Can you meet me with the letters and my other belongings? I shall be in the coach changing horses at the Antelope Hotel on Wednesday evening at half-past five. I still remain yours ever, LUCETTA.

Henchard took a deep breath and wished that he had never met Lucetta. On the day of the appointment, Henchard reached on time with Lucetta's belongings, but the coach was late. When it arrived, Lucetta was not in it. Henchard went home relieved, only to realise that Susan's condition was steadily deteriorating.

One day, Susan declared that she wanted to write something. She was given a pen, a piece of paper and a small desk was put on her bed. Then she was left alone. She wrote for a while and then sealed the paper writing on top,

To Mr Michael Henchard,

Not to be opened till Elizabeth-Jane's wedding day.

Then, Mrs Henchard confessed to Elizabeth-Jane that she had written two letters to both

Farfrae and her anonymously, asking them to meet each other.

"I wanted to bring the two of you together," she said. "I wanted Mr Farfrae to marry you."

"Oh, mother!" Elizabeth-Jane exclaimed. "Why?"

"I had a reason," Mrs Henchard replied. "You'll find out one day."

A little later, Farfrae passed by Henchard's house and, on an impulse, rang the bell. He was informed that Mrs Henchard had passed away just then.

Chapter Nine

The Revelation

After his wife's death, Henchard decided to tell Elizabeth-Jane that he was her real father and not Richard Newson. But he did not reveal the fact that he had sold them to Newson in a drunk state.

"What you witnessed was our second marriage. She married Newson after both of us thought that the other one was dead," Henchard added.

Elizabeth-Jane was distressed at this revelation and broke into tears. Henchard comforted her and she calmed down when she saw that he was equally sad.

"Will you agree to take my surname now?" Henchard asked her after she had believed his story and Elizabeth-Jane agreed. She wrote down the words that he dictated to her, which summed up that she would be hereby known as Elizabeth-Jane Henchard. Henchard dispatched the paper after sealing it to the offices of the *Casterbridge Chronicle*.

"I shall now fetch the documents that will prove that you are my daughter," Henchard said and went upstairs.

While looking for the papers, he discovered the note — not supposed to be opened before Elizabeth-Jane's wedding day — left behind by his late wife for him. But the seal of the letter had cracked open accidentally and Henchard read the now open letter. It went thus,

My Dear Michael,

I have kept a secret from you for the good of all three of us. Elizabeth-Jane is not your daughter. The child who was in my arms when you sold me

to Newson died three months later. This child is Newson's daughter and I christened her by the same name as she seemed to fill up the void that I had experienced owing to the loss of the earlier child.

Susan Henchard

Henchard was a superstitious man and was positive that the events of the day were reflective of some sinister plot against him to bring him down. In his mind, it appeared that someone was hell-bent on causing him pain by punishing him. But the irony was that everything had happened naturally. He would not have rummaged through his drawers for the papers if he had not shared his past with Elizabeth-Jane. It was a terrible mockery.

The minute he had revealed to Elizabeth-Jane that he was her father, he had found out that she was not his real daughter. Henchard left the house immediately and returned later only to spend a restless night.

The next morning, Elizabeth-Jane hooked her arms around his arms, affectionately at breakfast. "I believe everything that you said to me last night," she declared happily. "I shall not call you Mr Henchard now. Come father, breakfast is ready."

Henchard managed to kiss her cheek, but the truth was that he was now feeling miserable about the entire situation.

To Elizabeth-Jane, Henchard's aloofness was puzzling. He rebuked her for the slightest faults, like for using colloquial words or helping the women workers. One day, when Henchard learnt that Elizabeth-Jane often engaged in manual work, he was disgusted and felt that she was marring his reputation. Henchard had slowly developed an aversion to Elizabeth-Jane and scolded her at the slightest pretext.

One day, Elizabeth-Jane visited her mother's grave and saw a stranger reading the inscription on her mother's tombstone. The stranger was a lady in mourning, like Elizabeth-Jane, and was about her age and size. But she was better dressed than Elizabeth-Jane was. The stranger

left and Elizabeth-Jane approached the tomb and realised — on observing the footprints — that the stranger had stood there for a long time.

Elizabeth-Jane returned home to discover Henchard in a foul mood. His two-year term as the Mayor of Casterbridge was drawing to an end and he had just been informed that his name did not feature in the list of aldermen who were being considered for the post. He had also been told that Douglas Farfrae was likely to become a councillor.

Henchard had now realised that he had erred by not allowing Farfrae to communicate with Elizabeth-Jane. He wrote another letter to Farfrae, stating that he had no objection if he wished to court Elizabeth-Jane. But Henchard didn't want the business to be conducted in his own house.

The next day, Elizabeth-Jane visited the churchyard again and looked around for the woman who had visited her mother's grave. She spotted Farfrae instead, who disappeared

immediately. Although she was unsure if he had seen her, Elizabeth-Jane was seized by melancholy and sat down on a bench despondently.

"Oh, I wish I was dead with my mother," she said loudly.

"Whatever has happened, dear?" a voice startled her. It was the same lady, she had suddenly appeared. The two women started talking and Elizabeth-Jane opened her heart out to her new friend, and told her about the differences with her father.

"I gather from your words that he is a hot-tempered man," the lady said. "But there is no doubt that he also appears to be a good man."

Elizabeth-Jane found it strange that the lady was taking her side as well as taking pains not to disapprove of her father. She shared with her new friend the story of her life so far, but the lady was not as shocked as Elizabeth-Jane had expected her to be.

"Sometimes I wish I could leave his place and go somewhere else," Elizabeth-Jane confessed sadly. "But there is no place that I could go to."

"Things might get better soon," her new friend stated. "I would soon require a person to reside in my house, partly as a housekeeper and partly as my companion. Would this role suit you?" she asked Elizabeth-Jane.

"Yes," Elizabeth-Jane replied hopefully. "It would help me not to be dependent on my father and maybe then he might begin to love me."

"I have been residing at Budmouth while my house was getting ready in Casterbridge," the lady informed Elizabeth-Jane. "It is called the High-Place Hall and two to three rooms are now fit to be occupied, although it might take some time for the entire house to be ready. Please think over my proposal and meet me here on the first day of the next week. Let me know if you still want to move in with me then."

THE REVELATION

Elizabeth-Jane happily agreed to this kind proposal and the two women said goodbye at the churchyard gate.

Chapter Ten

Elizabeth-Jane Leaves Home

Elizabeth-Jane decided to visit High-Place Hall to have a look at the house. It had all the features of a typical country mansion and she saw lights in the upper rooms.

"The lady has obviously arrived," she concluded.

Suddenly, Elizabeth-Jane heard the sound of footsteps coming from the alley where she stood and retreated. She would have been surprised had she stayed and seen Henchard approach the house. But Elizabeth-Jane didn't and made her way home instead.

Henchard arrived home a little later and Elizabeth-Jane informed him about her decision

to leave home without divulging the details. Henchard made no objection, but offered her an allowance so that she wouldn't be inconvenienced living independently. The day to meet the lady arrived and Elizabeth-Jane met her at the appointed place.

"Have you arrived at a decision?" the lady asked her.

"Yes," she replied.

"Does your father agree?" she asked.

"Yes," Elizabeth-Jane said.

The lady asked Elizabeth-Jane to join her on that very day. "Have you informed your father where you are going?" she asked.

"No," she replied. "I thought it would be wiser to leave first as he possesses a temper that is unpredictable."

"Maybe you are right," the lady said. "I realise I haven't told you my name. It is Miss Templeman. I shall expect you at my house at six this evening then."

"Which way should I use to enter the house, ma'am?" Elizabeth-Jane enquired.

"The front way, around the gate," Miss Templeman replied. "There is no other way that I am aware of."

But Elizabeth-Jane was thinking about the door located in the alley.

Henchard reached home just before six and saw his step-daughter leaving with all her belongings.

"Where are you going?" a surprised Henchard asked.

"You gave me permission to leave, father," Elizabeth-Jane replied from the window of her carriage.

"But I thought you intended to do so next month, or perhaps next year," Henchard protested at the suddenness of her departure. "So, this is how you treat me after all that I've done for you. Well, do as you wish," Henchard said and stormed into the house.

He saw that all of her things had not been brought down yet and went to Elizabeth-Jane's room. The room was testimony to her orderliness, interest and desire for self up-gradation and enhancement. Books, sketches, maps and small, yet tasteful arrangements greeted Henchard, who returned downstairs immediately.

"Don't leave me," he said in a changed voice to Elizabeth-Jane. "I might have been rough in my speech towards you, but there is something that has caused me a lot of grief and I cannot share the same with you now. But if you stay with me and live here as my daughter, I promise to tell you all in due course."

"I think it is best for both of us if I leave now, father," Elizabeth-Jane replied kindly. "I am not headed too far away and can be back whenever you need me."

"Give me your address so that I may write to you if I wish to do so," Henchard demanded.

"High-Place Hall," Elizabeth-Jane replied as she waved to Henchard. He neither moved nor spoke as the carriage disappeared. Henchard was well aware that High-Place Hall was being

prepared for a lady tenant who went by the name of Templeman. He had also received a letter from Lucetta earlier announcing her plans to come and stay in Casterbridge.

In the letter, Lucetta had stated that she had decided to do so after learning about the death of his wife and would be able to meet him soon. Henchard had assumed that Lucetta was related to this lady named Templeman.

After Elizabeth-Jane's departure, Henchard received another letter from Lucetta. It said:

"My good Aunt Templeman, who was the widow of a banker, has passed away recently, bequeathing some of her property to me. I have taken her name to escape from mine and the scandal that follows it. I am now residing in High-Place Hall and I am my own mistress. You shall now not be inconvenienced in any manner if you choose to see me. You must be aware of the arrangement that I have made with your daughter. I met her purely by accident and you must see why I made this arrangement, Michael,

It is to give you the perfect excuse to come and see me on the pretext of visiting her without raising any eyebrows.

Yours always,

Lucetta

Henchard went to visit Lucetta but was told that Miss Templeman was busy that evening and would be happy to see him the next day.

'The woman thinks too much of herself,' Henchard thought as he left.

Meanwhile, Elizabeth-Jane had settled into her new home and learnt that Miss Templeman was originally from Jersey.

"In my native isle, they speak English on one side of the street and French on the other," Miss Templeman explained when Elizabeth-Jane asked her how she was fluent in both French and English.

Miss Templeman had also travelled a lot with her father, who was an officer in the army, but Bath was where her family originally hailed

from. After her father's death, she had lived in Jersey.

Lucetta waited for Henchard the next day, but he did not turn up.

On the day of the Candlemas fair, Lucetta sent Elizabeth-Jane out for an errand that would keep her occupied for a couple of hours. Then, she sent a note to Henchard asking him to visit her — he was supposed to be in the marketplace that was near her house with the other corn dealers on that day. Lucetta then waited till she heard a man's footsteps on the stairs. She flung back the curtain to greet Henchard. But the person before her was not Henchard.

Chapter Eleven

A Brand New Machine

The visitor at High-Place Hall was much younger than the Mayor of Casterbridge and was a handsome man. He was none other than Donald Farfrae.

"I'm sorry," he apologised to Lucetta. "I arrived to look for Miss Henchard and I was directed here. Have I come to the wrong house, madam?" he asked.

"Not at all, sir," Lucetta replied. "Please take a seat. Miss Henchard will be here shortly."

There was something appealing about Donald Farfrae, a quality that made him attractive to everyone instantly and even Lucetta succumbed to his charms. Farfrae had arrived to look for Elizabeth-Jane after Henchard had assured him through his letter that he had no objection if he met or courted his daughter. As Elizabeth-Jane had not arrived yet Lucetta struck up a conversation with the young man.

"I am clueless about how I should enjoy my riches," she said. "I arrived in Casterbridge hoping that it would be a likeable place to reside in. But I wonder if I shall actually like to live here. I am so lonely," she sighed.

"Where did you arrive from, ma'am?" Farfrae asked.

"Bath!"

"I'm from Edinburgh myself," Farfrae confessed. "While it's true that home is where the heart is, a man must live where he can make his money."

Lucetta surveyed him with more interest now and their gazes met.

"Do you wish to go back then?" she asked.

"No ma'am, I cannot afford to," he replied.

"I am just a struggling corn and hay merchant unlike a thriving person like you."

"I am also an ambitious woman," Lucetta replied.

"I almost forgot the business engagement I had," Farfrae stated suddenly but made no sign of leaving.

"You better leave or you shall lose a customer," Lucetta stated.

"You anger me now, Miss Templeman," Farfrae exclaimed.

"Then don't leave," she said. "Stay a little longer."

"I'm afraid I must leave as business cannot be neglected, right?" he said.

"Not for a second."

"May I come another time then?"

"Certainly," she replied. "What has happened between us today is very strange indeed. But whatever it was is now over. The market begs for your attention."

"I wish there were no markets," Farfrae replied.

"You should not change your views so suddenly," Lucetta said.

"This is the first time I am making such a wish," Farfrae replied. "It is only after seeing you."

"Then you shouldn't be seeing me, I fear I am demoralising you," she said.

"I shall see you in my thoughts then," Farfrae replied. "Thank you for the pleasure of this visit."

"Thank you for staying," she replied.

Sometime after Farfrae had left, the maid announced the Mayor.

"He says he doesn't have much time to spare today," the maid declared. "Tell him I won't keep him waiting either as I have a bad headache myself," Lucetta stated in dismissal.

Lucetta had arrived in Casterbridge to rekindle her relationship with Henchard. Now that the feat had been achieved, she was getting indifferent to the same.

"I'm so happy you've come," Lucetta said when Elizabeth-Jane returned. "I do hope that you stay with me for a long time."

She thought it was a novel idea, to have Elizabeth-Jane as a watch-dog to keep her father away.

Lucetta's house had the advantage of offering a direct view of the marketplace; a view that both the women enjoyed.

One day, they saw a strange looking vehicle come to a standstill at the marketplace. It was a newly-invented agricultural instrument called the horse drill and its arrival created a sensation in Casterbridge. It was as if a flying machine had chosen to land at Charing Cross. Men, women and children all flocked to catch a glimpse of the unknown machine painted a merry green, yellow and red.

"Why, it looks like an agricultural piano," Lucetta said to Elizabeth-Jane as they joined the crowd.

"Good morning, Elizabeth-Jane," Henchard greeted her suddenly.

"Good morning, father," Elizabeth-Jane replied. "This is Miss Templeman, the lady I'm living with."

Henchard touched his hat in greeting as Lucetta bowed.

"I am pleased to make your acquaintance, Mr Henchard," she said. "What a strange-looking machine this is."

Henchard agreed and explained the workings of the machine, marking its efficiency as well.

"But who brought it here?" Lucetta enquired.

"It was brought here by a machinist on the recommendation of a fool who thinks...," Henchard paused and turned to leave. He quickly whispered to Lucetta, "You refused to see me," but Elizabeth-Jane had heard him.

Then he strode away from the women into the market house. The two women turned towards the corn drill now and saw the back of a man, humming a cheerful tune, bent over the machine in an attempt to master its secrets.

"It looks like a wonderful new drill," Lucetta addressed the man.

Farfrae turned around and replied, "This machine will revolutionise the concept of sowing here. There will be no more sowers throwing their seeds after broadcast and no more loss of seeds when they are thrown. Each grain will end up where it is intended to."

"Does the machine belong to you?" Lucetta asked.

"No ma'am," Farfrae replied. "It was just brought here on my recommendation."

After meeting Farfrae again and observing his behaviour towards Miss Templeman, Elizabeth-Jane could not help but think how friendly the two of them appeared to be.

Chapter Twelve

Henchard Gets Desperate

Farfrae now came to meet Lucetta instead of Elizabeth-Jane, but he also pretended to converse with her. Elizabeth-Jane digested this cold treatment; she had after all been conditioned to bear with worse things in life. As soon as Farfrae came for his visit to High-Place Hall, she found excuses to exit the room quickly and at the slightest opportunity. With each passing day, the relationship between Lucetta and Farfrae became stronger.

But one day, Henchard visited Lucetta and offered to marry her. However, Lucetta declined and Henchard left in a hurry.

"I will not love him anymore," Lucetta decided. "It would be madness to bind myself to one who is so strict and hot-tempered. I shall not be enslaved to my past and will choose my own man to love."

Elizabeth-Jane had witnessed her father and Donald Farfrae fight to win Miss Templeman's affections and felt sad as Farfrae had been her undeclared lover. Henchard spoke to him about Lucetta the next time their paths crossed. But Farfrae refused to stop seeing her.

One day, Farfrae arrived while Henchard was sitting with Lucetta, making him very suspicious. Their hostess offered them bread and butter in long slices and each man grabbed the slice she held out, thinking it was intended for him. Neither would let go and soon the slice was broken into two parts, leaving the two men in a silly situation. Angry, Henchard left the house, though he had no proof that Farfrae and Lucetta were lovers. But there was no doubt in Elizabeth-Jane's mind that this was the truth.

Henchard decided to take matters in his own hand and sent for Jopp, who had replaced Farfrae as his manager.

"As the biggest corn and hay dealer in these parts, it is important for me that Scot suffer losses," he instructed Jopp. "By fair competition, of course." he added. "He is venturing into my trade in town and I have decided to crush him with the capital at my disposal."

Then, till late in the evening, he shared with Jopp his precise plan for putting Farfrae out of business.

Elizabeth-Jane, who had accidentally come to know about Jopp being hired by Henchard, tried to persuade Henchard not to do so, but he silenced her with a sharp rebuke.

The season was just right for Henchard to execute his plan. The weather was bad and it was also perfect for his little scheme.

This was a time before the grain trade was revolutionised by international trade. The wheat quotations then were still dependent

upon the domestic harvest on a monthly basis. A bad harvest, or even the prospect of one, could double the price of corn in a matter of a few weeks just as the prospect of a good harvest could lower it considerably.

Henchard predicted a disastrous harvest and was backed by Jopp. But Henchard was a superstitious man and he wanted to back his assumption with solid facts and visited a weather clairvoyant living on the outskirts of town.

"The last fortnight of August will witness heavy rain," the man predicted.

"Are you sure?" Henchard enquired.

"As sure in a world where everything is unsure," the clairvoyant replied.

The very next Saturday, Henchard purchased a massive amount of grain so that the people of Casterbridge spoke about this huge purchase for the next couple of days. Henchard's granaries were bursting at their seams, but he had made a grave error in his calculations. The weather

changed suddenly and an excellent harvest was almost a certainty now. The prices surged downwards. Henchard was shocked, but it was too late to back out now. His purchases had been great and to settle his debts, he was forced to sell corn at a much lower price than he had purchased. Henchard faced heavy losses and sacked Jopp because of his wrong advice.

"You shall be sorry for this, Sir," Jopp threatened before he left.

On the eve of the harvest, Farfrae purchased heavily as prices were low. If only Henchard had exercised some patience, he would not have suffered losses. Certain that some invisible power was conspiring against him, Henchard sold off everything in a mad rush. On the other hand, Donald Farfrae prospered as he had invested sensibly in a depressed market and had made a killing when prices were moderate again.

'That man might be made Mayor,' Henchard thought jealously.

Henchard was refused entry when he visited Lucetta's house again as the lady had a prior engagement. Henchard lurked in the shadows outside to spot Farfrae arrive and knock on the door. Lucetta opened the door herself and they walked out together. Henchard decided to follow them keeping a safe distance. After some time, they stopped at a desolate place and Henchard hid in such a manner that he could eavesdrop on their conversation.

"Say what you wish to," Lucetta announced gaily.

"You must be sought after by men for your wealth, beauty, talent and position in society," Farfrae began. "But wouldn't you be satisfied with only one admirer in your home instead of many?" he asked.

"Are you talking about yourself?" Lucetta laughed. "Are you certain my many admirers won't make you jealous?"

"No," he replied as he held her hand.

They walked together for some time before Lucetta excused herself and started to return home alone. Henchard followed her home and met her in her sitting room. He threatened Lucetta saying that if she did not agree to marry him he would reveal the details of their secret relationship to everyone.

Lucetta immediately sent for Elizabeth-Jane.

Henchard took his daughter's hand and said, "I want you to hear this, Elizabeth-Jane," then he turned to Lucetta and added, "Will you marry me or not?"

Lucetta agreed reluctantly and immediately after that, she lost consciousness.

"What forces her to agree to your proposal, father, when it is evident that it is causing her so much pain?" Elizabeth-Jane demanded of Henchard. She knelt by Lucetta's side and urged her father not to force Miss Templeman into doing something that she did not want.

"You are a simpleton," Henchard scolded his step-daughter. "Don't you realise that her marriage to me will leave him free to marry you? Don't you want him?"

Lucetta rose from her stupor at this statement and exclaimed, "Him? Who are you talking about?"

"No one as far as I'm concerned," Elizabeth-Jane replied.

"I must be mistaken," Henchard admitted. "But Miss Templeman here has agreed to be my wife now!"

"Michael, I will not marry you and that's final," Lucetta insisted.

Henchard left and Elizabeth-Jane asked Lucetta what power her father held over her.

"You called him Michael as if you have known him for a while," she exclaimed. "How could you promise to marry him before if your heart was not set upon him? I fear you have kept too many secrets from me, Miss Templeman."

"Maybe you have kept some from me as well," Lucetta mumbled.

"I cannot imagine causing you pain like this," Elizabeth-Jane stated. "I fail to comprehend how my father can make such demands from you. Maybe I should go and have a word with him."

"No," Lucetta said. "Let it be."

Chapter Thirteen

The Trial of the Furmity Woman

Henchard attended Petty Sessions in the Town Hall the next morning as he was still a magistrate on account of his late position as Mayor. Dr Chalkfield, the Mayor for the year, was absent and so Henchard took the chair.

There was only one case, of an old woman causing nuisance and disorder. When the charges against the old woman had been read, it was time for her to speak in her defence.

"It was 20 years ago," she began. "I was selling furmity in a tent at Weydon Fair when a man, woman and a child entered. I used to season my furmity with rum for people who asked for it and the man kept asking for more. Then, after he had many of them, he argued with his wife and put her up for sale to the highest bidder. A sailor bought his wife for five guineas and took her away. The man who sold his wife is none other than the man sitting on that high chair," the woman pointed towards Henchard. "That proves that he is no better than I am and has no right to pronounce judgment upon me."

"Her story is concocted," the clerk protested.

"No, it is true," Henchard stated and rose from his chair. "It proves that I am no better than her and hence, I leave the chair."

The story spread like wildfire across Casterbridge. Lucetta heard about it for the first time. She became depressed when she recalled how Henchard had been persistent in his efforts to marry her and decided to leave Casterbridge for a while. She retired to the seaside of Port-Bredy leaving Elizabeth-Jane to take care of High-Place Hall. Henchard visited her house only to learn that she had left.

Lucetta was travelling towards Port-Bredy with great speed and after having walked a mile or so, she stopped and sighed.

"Oh Donald!" she whispered.

Suddenly, she spotted a figure approaching her. It was Elizabeth-Jane.

"It struck me suddenly that I should come and see you," she smiled and explained. Elizabeth-Jane did not notice a bull charging at her from behind. Lucetta grabbed her arm and ran as the two ladies sought refuge in the nearby barn. But the bull followed them inside the barn and the ladies were terrified.

Suddenly, a man appeared and grabbed the bull's head expertly. Twisting the bull's head by its horns, the man managed to subdue it and led the animal outside the barn.

It was none other than Henchard and Lucetta started to weep hysterically. Henchard returned to carry her outside in his arms. Lucetta suddenly recalled that she had left her muff behind in the barn and Elizabeth-Jane ran

back to fetch it. She was returning when she saw Farfrae drive up in a rig. It was now clear to Elizabeth-Jane why Lucetta had chosen to walk out this way. Farfrae stopped on seeing Elizabeth-Jane and she briefed him about the events. Farfrae was surprised that Henchard had saved their lives and was taking Lucetta home. But Henchard wanted to take Lucetta to his creditor, Mr Grower instead. He intended to delay the repayment of his loan to Mr Grower using his supposed marriage to Lucetta as an excuse. But Henchard's surprise knew no bounds when he came to know that Lucetta had already married Farfrae that very week at Port-Bredy. Ironically, Mr Grower had been the witness.

"How could I marry you after I had learnt that you had sold your first wife?" Lucetta stated to Henchard.

"I had saved his wife's life," Henchard said.

"He shall be indebted to you forever for that," Lucetta replied.

"You liar!" Henchard exclaimed. "You broke your promise to me."

"You forced me to," Lucetta cried. "Besides, I was unaware of your murky past."

"You should be punished, you deserve to be," Henchard stated threateningly. "Your precious happiness shall end with one word to your husband about to how you courted me and the details of our past."

"Oh no, Michael!" Lucetta exclaimed. "Pray, have some pity on me," she begged.

"You don't deserve any pity," Henchard shouted.

"I can help you repay all your debts," Lucetta offered.

"I refuse to accept charity from Farfrae's wife of all people," Henchard said disdainfully. "Go away!"

Lucetta reached home quickly and gave the news to the servants about her husband's arrival. Farfrae arrived half an hour later.

"I haven't broken the news of our marriage to Elizabeth-Jane yet," she said to him.

"I dropped her home from the barn but I did not tell her either," Farfrae replied.

"You don't mind if she continues living with me, do you Donald?" she asked.

"Of course, I don't." he replied.

"I'll go and tell her," Lucetta stated.

When Lucetta told her about the marriage, Elizabeth-Jane asked Lucetta to give her some time to think about it. Lucetta assured that both she and her new husband wanted her to stay with them.

But the truth was that Susan Henchard's daughter had already made up her mind to quit Lucetta's employment. Lucetta had not taken her into confidence regarding her plans to marry Farfrae and she was hurt by this betrayal. Besides, Farfrae and her had once shown interest in each other. She could not bear to stay with them on any account. It was early evening when Elizabeth-Jane packed all

her belongings and moved out of the house. She had become very resourceful and had had no trouble finding an accommodation. But she realised that she would have to live in a very economical manner now.

Elizabeth-Jane wrote a farewell note to Lucetta. Then, she called a man with a barrow, put her boxes in it and trotted over to her rooms, which incidentally were right opposite Henchard's residence. Elizabeth-Jane had calculated that the allowance bestowed on her by her father would help her survive. She had also picked up the wonderful skill of netting as a child, which would hold her in good stead now. Her education, which she had pursued with zeal and without any cost, would also help her make money.

Chapter Fourteen

The Fall of Henchard

All of Casterbridge now knew about the furmity woman's revelation and although the incident at the court had been small, it brought about a downslide in Henchard's fortunes — both socially and economically. The debtor he had trusted blindly did not pay him back and his credit was escalating rapidly. Henchard had become a desperate man and failed to contain the strict correspondence between bulk and sample, which is a necessity in the commerce of grain.

One of his men was entirely responsible for this debacle as he had unwisely taken possession of the sample of a mammoth quantity of second-rate corn Henchard had held and removed the pinched, blasted and smutted grain in vast numbers. Even if this produce had been honestly sold, no scandal would have been forthcoming. But Henchard's name was spoilt on account of this blunder.

The timing could not have been worse.

Elizabeth-Jane was moved to tears one day when she came to know that the commissioners were meeting to discuss Henchard's bankruptcy. The creditors refused to accept Henchard's personal belongings, like the gold watch he offered them, although the senior commissioner admitted that he had never encountered a debtor who was as fair as Henchard. Despite Henchard's reputation and the general feeling to condemn him, there was a wave of sympathy for him in Casterbridge when all his belongings were ticketed and put to auction. Elizabeth-Jane tried her best but could not manage to meet him. But she had believed in him when no one else had and she also forgave him for his behaviour towards her.

Henchard did not reply when she wrote to him and neither did she find him when she visited his house. The ex-mayor was living as a tenant now in Jopp's house, the very Jopp whom he had employed, coaxed, threatened, used and then dismissed. But Henchard was not to be found there as well.

More bad news followed. Elizabeth-Jane learnt that Donald Farfrae was now the master of Henchard's hay-barns and corn-stores.

One day, Jopp informed Henchard that Farfrae and his wife had moved into Henchard's old house and that the fellow who had bought all of Henchard's furniture had actually bought it on behalf of Farfrae.

"My house and then my furniture?" Henchard exclaimed in despair. "What will he buy next? My body and soul?"

"He certainly will if you wish to sell them," Jopp replied. Satisfied that he had inflicted a

deep wound in his old master's heart, Jopp left Henchard alone on the stone bridge where they had met.

After some time, Henchard saw a rig appear on the bridge that was headed towards town. It was Farfrae.

"I have heard that you are thinking of leaving town, Mr Henchard," he said.

"Yes, I am leaving, just like you. Once you had wanted to leave town and I stopped you," Henchard replied. "Isn't it strange how circumstances have reversed now?"

"Yes, that is the way of the world," Farfrae replied. "I have a proposition for you if you care to listen. Come back and live in your old house till you find an opening for yourself. We can spare a few rooms for you and I'm sure that my wife won't object."

"No!" Henchard replied roughly, shocked at the very idea.

"It will be a much healthier accommodation than the quarters by the river you are residing

in currently," Farfrae offered generously. "You shall have a part of the house to yourself without anybody disturbing you."

But Henchard refused to accept the generous offer. The two men walked in the town together and Farfrae offered some supper to Henchard in his house who refused again.

"I have purchased some of your furniture," Farfrae informed Henchard. "It is not that I wanted to possess it. But I ensured that I purchased the ones that you cherished so you could take them to your new house."

"You paid money for it. So, why would you let me have the furniture for nothing?" a surprised Henchard asked.

"Well, the truth is that you value them more than I would," Farfrae replied. Henchard was moved.

"I often think that I have wronged you," he said and shook Farfrae's hand suddenly. Then, as if ashamed of having displayed his emotions, he rushed away.

Soon, news reached Elizabeth-Jane that Henchard had caught cold and was bound to his room. She left to see him immediately and found him sitting on the bed with a big coat wrapped around him. Henchard was initially averse to her intrusion, but Elizabeth-Jane stayed despite his protests. She made both him and the room more comfortable, instructed the people living below and had won the affection of her stepfather by the time she left.

Henchard's thoughts were more about Elizabeth-Jane now than about leaving Casterbridge. One day, he made an important decision that revolved around the fact that there was nothing to be ashamed about and good honest work. Encouraged by the fact that Farfrae was a much better man than he had given him credit for, Henchard strode into Farfrae's yard and offered his services as a journeyman hay-trusser. His application was accepted instantly. The once Mayor of Casterbridge and a thriving merchant was thus reduced to a common

labourer in the very barns and granaries that had once belonged to him.

"I have worked as a journeyman before, haven't I?" he would state in his defence. "There is no reason why I shouldn't be employed as one again."

Winter soon approached and rumours started doing the rounds in Casterbridge that Farfrae's name was being proposed for the post of mayor, election for which was supposed to take place in a couple of years. He was already a member of the Town Council.

Gradually, Henchard's character experienced a moral transformation. He could be heard saying, "Only a fortnight more! I have to wait for only twelve days now!"

"Why do you have to wait for 12 days?" a co-worker enquired.

"I shall be free from my oath in another 12 days," Henchard explained. "In 12 days, I shall be free to drink again as it will be 21 years since I swore not to consume alcohol. It is then that I shall enjoy myself fully, so help me God!"

Chapter Fifteen

Letters from Lucetta

A sociable custom existed in Casterbridge. Every Sunday afternoon, a large group of the Casterbridge journeymen who were regular churchgoers and men of good character, mingled with each other at The Three Mariners after attending the service. The choir brought about the rear of this contingent, armed with fiddles, bass-viols and flutes. The point of honour in this sacred gathering was for every man to limit himself to not more than half a pint of liquor.

It so happened that The Three Mariners was Henchard's chosen venue as well to break his

oath of being a teetotaller. Henchard had timed his entry so that he was already seated in the huge room by the time the 40 odd churchgoers had entered for their customary drink. From Henchard's expression it was clear that a new era of drunken recklessness was promising to begin afresh.

Elizabeth-Jane also entered the room at this time having heard of her stepfather's decision to break his vow. Her worried eyes sought out Henchard and as the choir and the company exited, she approached Henchard and begged him to accompany her home. He hadn't drunk a great quantity and she persuaded him to come with her.

"I am a man who has kept his word," Henchard said to Elizabeth-Jane after some time. "I have not broken my oath for 21 years and I can drink with a clear conscience now. He has robbed me of everything I possessed and if I meet him I shall not answer for my deeds," he stated with conviction.

Elizabeth-Jane was alarmed at this half-stated disclosure.

"What do you have in mind?" she asked fearfully, but Henchard did not reply. Neither did he permit her to enter his cottage when they reached. Elizabeth-Jane left, thinking it was her duty to warn Farfrae.

She woke up the next morning at the crack of dawn and met Farfrae at Corn Street.

"Why is Miss Henchard up so early?" he asked.

"I am eager to tell you something," Elizabeth-Jane stated. "I did not want to alarm Mrs Farfrae by coming to the house."

She then told Farfrae about her suspicion that her father might be driven to injure him. Farfrae made light of her fears as he thought he faced no danger from Henchard. Joyce advised Farfrae to dismiss Henchard from his employ.

"I cannot do that as he was once a good friend to me," Farfrae said, dismissively. "It was he who helped me gain a solid footing in this town."

He also said that if the people wanted him to become the Mayor, he would not disappoint them, no matter how much Henchard raved and ranted about it.

Lucetta was uneasy for a different reason altogether.

"Michael, please return any letters or papers of mine that you have in your possession," she pleaded with Henchard when she came across him, accidentally. "I had asked you to do so months ago."

Henchard had actually packed all of Lucetta's letters but had not delivered them. He recalled that the packet lay among a heap of useless papers in a safe in the dining room of his old house. Ironically, unknown to Lucetta, her letters and papers were in the very house in which she resided now.

Henchard allowed himself a smile, which was pure evil. 'Had Farfrae opened the safe?'

That very evening, a massive ringing of bells in Casterbridge proclaimed that Donald Farfrae had been elected Mayor, the 200th odd member of an elective dynasty that could be traced back to the days of Charles I. Henchard met Farfrae the next morning.

"I meant to ask you about a packet belonging to me that I have left in the safe of my dining room," Henchard stated.

"If you have left it there, then, still you'll there it as I haven't opened the safe," Farfrae replied.

"It is not that important to me," Henchard said. "But I'll come for it later today if you don't mind?"

Farfrae agreed and Henchard arrived rather late in the evening. Farfrae invited him into the dining room, where he unlocked the safe and handed over the papers to Henchard with an apology for not having returned them earlier.

"Never mind. These are mostly letters," Henchard replied as he opened the bundle that bore testimony to Lucetta's passion. "Of course, you recall that strange chapter in my life that I had once mentioned to you. You had helped

me out then by writing a letter. These letters are linked to that unhappy event. Thank God, it's a thing of the past now."

"But whatever happened to that unfortunate woman?" Farfrae asked.

"She married and luckily, she married well," Henchard replied and then started reading a few lines aloud from Lucetta's letters. Then he and Farfrae started speaking about the woman.

Henchard's initial plan was to create a grand calamity at the end of these theatrics by reading out Lucetta's name at the end of the letter. He had arrived at Farfrae's house with no other objective in mind other than that. But now, he discovered that he could not bring himself to do it.

Lucetta had retired early to bed. But she could not sleep and instead, sat in the bedside chair, trying to read as she mulled the events of the day. When the doorbell had rung, she wondered who had called at this late hour. She left her room and slowly descended the stairs

and by the time she reached the lower flight of the stairs, she could hear the two men talking. She froze as her own written words greeted her ears in Henchard's voice. Lucetta fled to her bedroom, absolutely shocked, but when she returned after Henchard's departure, she was surprised to see Farfrae smiling at her as if he'd been rid of a bothersome pest.

The next morning, Lucetta remained in bed, trying to figure out a way to counter Henchard's unexpected assault. She decided that the only way was to try and persuade the enemy.

Picking up a pen and paper, she wrote to Henchard,

I overheard part of your conversation with my husband last night and saw the extent you could go to extract revenge upon me. The very thought breaks me down. Please have pity on a woman who is suffering so much. If only you could see me, you would yield. I shall be present at the Ring when you leave from work just before sunset. I shall know no

*peace until I have seen you face to face and have heard
from your own mouth that you shall not carry this
tomfoolery any further.*

Lucetta did not sign off with her name in
order to avoid recognition and slipped out
of the house silently at the appointed hour.
Eventually, Henchard arrived but stood away
from her confusing Lucetta. But the truth
was that her forlorn figure in that massive
enclosure, the uncharacteristic plainness of her
clothes and her demeanour of hope and prayer
brought back the memory of another woman in
Henchard's life, a woman he had wronged. He
remembered Susan who was now in her grave.
His conscience reprimanded him severely for
attacking this woman. He came to stand in front
of Lucetta and asked her in a kind voice, "What
do you want me to do?"

"To get back the letters and papers which are
in your possession," Lucetta replied.

"So be it," Henchard replied and promised
to send them over the next morning.

But the next morning, before Lucetta could go to get the letters from Henchard, Jopp arrived to seek a favour. He said he had offered his services to Farfrae, in a letter earlier, and wished to be a working partner. He wanted Lucetta to put in a good word for him. Lucetta coldly replied that it was none of her business and refused to help him.

"I happened to be in Jersey for many years ma'am and I have seen you there," Jopp said.

"But I know nothing about you," Lucetta stated.

Jopp pleaded with her but she refused to do his bidding.

When Jopp returned home, Henchard asked him to deliver a sealed package to Farfrae. Jopp was extremely curious about the contents of the package and wondered what it could contain that prevented Henchard from delivering it personally.

En route, he opened one of the seals with his penknife and saw that the package contained

letters. He resealed it and went his way. Jopp had to cross the river-side at the base of the town. He spotted Mother Cuxsom and Nance Mockridge near the bridge at the end of High Street. This was near Mixen Lane where waifs, strays and vagabonds lived. The landlady, however, was a good woman who had been unjustly sent to prison many years ago. She had set up a house after her prison term and was friendly with these people. Jopp and his acquaintances arrived at the house and spoke about old times.

"It is not our greatest doings that the world is aware of," the old furmity woman said. She was the latest member to have settled here.

"But the grand secret is nothing but the passion of love," Jopp stated. "How can a woman love one man so passionately and yet hate another so dreadfully?"

"Who are you talking about, sir?"

"Someone who is regarded in this town and someone I'd surely like to shame," Jopp replied.

"I'd love to read her love letters. Why, it would be like watching a play unfold before my eyes. You see, it's nothing but her love letters that I'm carrying."

"Love letters?" exclaimed Mother Cuxsom. "Let's hear them then, my good man!"

Jopp needed no urging as he opened the seals and took out the letters. He began to read aloud and slowly, the secret that Lucetta had been so frantic to conceal was revealed.

"Oh, Mrs Farfrae wrote that?" Nance Mockridge exclaimed. "It is indeed humbling for us women, knowing that respectable women like her are capable of such acts. Now she has given herself to another man!"

"It was a sensible decision by her," the old furmity woman insisted. "I was the one who saved her from a really bad marriage and yet she never thanked me once."

"It's such a good enough reason for a skimmity-ride, I say," Nance said and Mrs Cuxsom agreed with her that this opportunity should not go to waste.

"Why, the last time someone's effigy was paraded for immoral behaviour in Casterbridge must have been almost 10 years ago," she reflected. Someone blew a shrill whistle then and the landlady addressed a man, "Jim is coming in, Charl. Would you mind going and letting down the bridge?"

Charl and his mate Joe rose and took a lantern from the landlady. They exited from the back door down the garden path that ended at the edge of the stream.

"Whatever is a skimmity-ride?" Jopp asked.

"Well, sir," the landlady replied. "It's an old practice in these parts to castigate a wife's immoral behaviour. But I don't approve of such things as a respectable landlady."

"But are they going to do it?" Jopp demanded. "It must be a good sight, I think?"

"It's a funny sight," she replied, obviously delighted at the thought of a skimmity-ride. "But it costs money."

"Well, good folks!" Jopp declared. "I'd like to take a look at this old custom that you spoke of and I don't mind contributing to a noble cause," he said and threw a sovereign on the table. The sovereign was collected and given to the landlady for safekeeping.

"There's more where that came from," Charl stated.

"Let's get the business started first," Jopp replied.

"We will," Nance said.

Jopp collected the letters and since it was rather late, he didn't bother to deliver them that night. He went home and sealed the letters again. Jopp delivered the package the following morning and its contents were burnt immediately by Lucetta, who fell to her knees in relief and thankfulness that all the evidence that linked her past with Henchard had been successfully destroyed.

Chapter Sixteen

The Demonic Sabbath

A Royal Personage was due to pass through Casterbridge to inaugurate a big engineering project further west. He had agreed to halt at Casterbridge for half an hour and was supposed to receive an address from the town corporation. The Town Council had met a day prior to his arrival to discuss the details of the event. Henchard entered the room, dressed in his primitive shabby clothes that he used to don when he was a labourer.

"I'd like to join you in welcoming our royal visitor," he announced.

"I hardly think that would be appropriate, Mr Henchard," the young Mayor, Farfrae objected.

But on the day, Henchard surprised everybody by appearing at the venue wearing a splendid rosette, carrying a homemade flag. But he was still wearing his battered, worn out clothes while everybody was attend in new clothes — right from the Mayor to the washerwoman.

Elizabeth-Jane watched along with the others as the Royal cortége approached. To her surprise, she spotted Henchard standing on the road. He approached the side of the slowing vehicle before anyone could stop him. With his left hand, he waved the Union Jack while he extended his right hand to the Royal Personage. He was held and suddenly dragged back by the shoulder, by Mayor Farfrae, who had decided to take matters in his own hands.

For an instant, Henchard stood his ground stubbornly and then slunk off slowly. The Royal Personage had noticed the incident but was tactful enough not to mention it. He got off the vehicle, the Mayor moved towards him and the address was read. The Royal Personage spoke to Farfrae after that. Then he shook hands with Lucetta, the Mayor's wife. Amidst a section of the crowd, few people spoke about the impending skimmity-ride that they had planned.

"Tonight!" Jopp declared to the Peter's party at one end of the Mixen Lane. "It will be the perfect wind-up to the Royal visit as the hit will be well-timed," Jopp laughed.

But he was not joking; it was all about revenge for him.

Lucetta was thrilled that the Royal Personage had shaken her hand, though it had been a brief encounter. Henchard had withdrawn silently and was shocked when he heard Lucetta speak to the other ladies, denying that Henchard had ever helped Donald. She stated that Henchard was just a common journeyman. Jopp met him and tried to gain his confidence by saying that they had both been snubbed and had a common enemy. But Henchard ignored him and moved on to Farfrae's house. He left a message for Farfrae to meet him in the granaries.

He threw a challenge at Farfrae when he arrived, "Let us finish that wrestle you began in this four-square loft," Henchard proposed. "The door is 40 feet above the ground. The one who manages to throw out the other from that door is the winner. He might state that the other has fallen out by accident or tell the truth. The choice is up to him. As I'm stronger than you, I have tied one arm to give you an equal footing in the match."

Farfrae did not have any time to agree or refuse as Henchard charged at him. Each man grabbed the other by the collar and the struggle for survival went on for a long time. Finally, Henchard had the upper hand and managed to get Farfrae right on the edge of the precipice.

Soon, Farfrae's head hung over the windowsill and one of his arms dangled outside the wall.

"This is the end, my friend," Henchard gasped. "It's time to end what you started this morning. Your life is in my hands."

"Then take it," Farfrae exclaimed. "God knows you've wanted to do so for a long time now."

Henchard stared at him silently for a while before he protested, "That's not true at all, Farfrae. God is witness that I've not loved any man as dearly as you. I came to kill you today, but I know that I cannot hurt you in any manner. Go and charge me with whatever offence you want to. I simply do not care what happens to me anymore," Henchard said and flung himself into a corner, remorsefully.

Farfrae observed him silently and then exited.

Farfrae's men were aware of the hideous plan by the residents of Mixen Lane and decided to send him out of town so he would not witness the horrible event. Whittle carried an anonymous letter which they had written

to Farfrae, demanding Farfrae's presence at Weatherbury on urgent business. Farfrae was a little shaken by his battle with Henchard and decided to leave at once to get it out of his mind. But Henchard overheard his plans.

Lucetta was sitting in the dining room alone that night, in a rather buoyant mood. For her, the day had been a success.

Her pleasant reverie was interrupted by a great commotion outside, and the noise became louder with each passing minute.

The voice of a maidservant standing near an upper window across the street speaking to another maid drew Lucetta's attention.

"Where are they headed now?" the first maid enquired eagerly.

"They are coming up Corn Street sitting back-to-back," was the reply.

"What? Are there two figures?" the maid asked. "How do they look?"

"Yes, there are two stuffed figures with false faces placed back-to-back on a donkey with their elbows tied together. He is facing the donkey's tail while she faces the head. The man is dressed in a blue coat and kerseymere leggings. He has a reddish face and black whiskers."

"What about the woman?"

"Her hair is in bands with the back-comb in place. Her neck is uncovered and she's wearing a puce silk, white stockings and coloured shoes."

Lucetta jumped to her feet and at that very moment the door opened and Elizabeth-Jane walked in. She quickly closed the window shutters as Lucetta rushed by her side to restrain her.

"It is me," she cried to Elizabeth-Jane and her face was as white as death.

"Let us shut the window," Elizabeth-Jane gently said.

"It is useless," Lucetta exclaimed. "Donald will spot it on his way home and will be heartbroken. He'll stop loving me and that will be the end of me!"

"Can't we stop it somehow?" Elizabeth-Jane asked, panic king. "Can no one stop this? Please let me shut the window," she pleaded.

"That is me, to the very last breath," Lucetta shrieked and then laughed like a maniac. "Why, she's even wearing my green parasol."

She then fell unconscious and fell on the floor. Elizabeth-Jane rang the doorbell repeatedly but none of the servants appeared as they had all run out to witness the Demonic Sabbath. The doctor was finally fetched and he declared that Lucetta's condition was serious.

"Send for Mr Farfrae at once," he ordered.

A man was dispatched immediately to fetch the Mayor as the magistrate, Benjamin Grower, got in touch with the constables.

"What can the two of us do against such a huge crowd?" Stubberd, the constable complained to Grower.

"Find out the names of the perpetrators immediately," Grower ordered but as if by

magic, the effigies, lanterns, the band and the donkey had all vanished in thin air.

A determined Grower sent out men to find the perpetrators. Henchard had seen the procession as well and was shocked. He immediately visited Elizabeth-Jane's residence and was informed that she was at Farfrae's residence. He went there at once to learn what had happened and that Farfrae's men had left to meet him on the Budmouth Road.

"But he has gone to Weatherbury and not towards Budmouth," Henchard protested.

Sadly, Henchard's reputation was now in ruins and no one believed him. No messenger was sent to Weatherbury even though Lucetta's life absolutely depended on her husband's immediate return. A frustrated Henchard decided to find Farfrae himself and he set off immediately. He reached the end of town to spot the lights of Farfrae's gig in the distance. Henchard stopped Farfrae and told him about Lucetta's illness, but Farfrae refused to believe

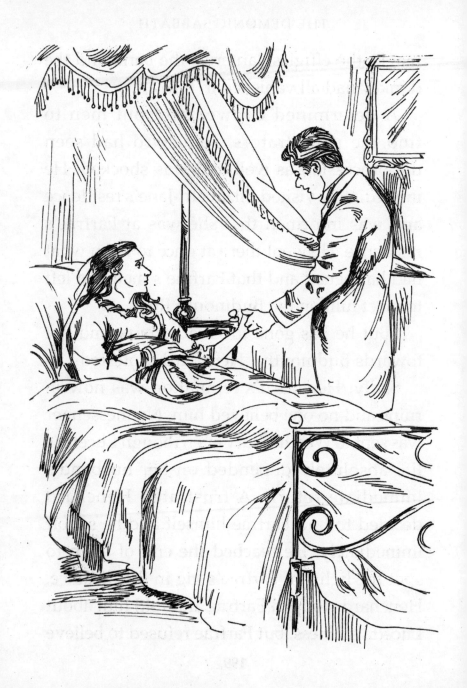

him and moved on. Farfrae reached home and was confused when he realised that Henchard had been speaking the truth. Farfrae could not comprehend the true nature of the man.

Lucetta recovered a little once her husband arrived and Farfrae spent the night by her bedside. Lucetta tried to tell him her terrible secret that night, but he silenced her; talking was not advisable in her fragile condition. Farfrae was still ignorant of the dreadful parade, though the serious illness and Lucetta's miscarriage had already become the talk of the town.

It remained Farfrae's secret as to how much his wife told him about her romantic liaison with Henchard that night. However, the watchman saw a man walk up and down Corn Street the entire night.

The man was none other than Henchard, who had made enquiries about Lucetta's health every now and then. Henchard's last call was made at four in the morning. He saw the servant

open the door quietly and untie the piece of cloth that had been used to muffle the sound of the door knocker.

"Why are you taking that off?" Henchard demanded.

The servant recognised Henchard and mournfully replied, "Because one may knock as loudly as one can, but she will never hear it anymore."

Chapter Seventeen

Newson Arrives

Henchard returned home and later Elizabeth-Jane came to give him the news of Lucetta's death that he was already aware of. Soon, there was another knock on his door and Henchard found himself face-to-face with a well-built man.

"Good morning! Am I speaking with Mr Henchard?" he asked.

"Yes," Henchard replied, showing the stranger in after he requested that he wanted a word with Henchard.

"Do you remember me?" he asked and Henchard shook his head.

"My name is Newson," the stranger replied and Henchard was stunned.

Newson continued, "I have been searching for you for a long time. I came to know that you were residing in Casterbridge and so I came here. I asked for directions and they showed me where you lived. I came to see you about that transaction we had 20 years ago. It was a strange business."

"Strange?" Henchard exclaimed. "It was worse than that! I was not in my right mind."

"We were both young and reckless," Newson concluded. "But I've arrived to make amends rather than open past wounds. Poor Susan! She had the strangest experience!"

"She was a simple, warm-hearted woman and lacked shrewdness," Henchard offered and Newson agreed.

"You must be aware that she thought the transaction to be legal," Newson stated. "She was as innocent as an angel in the skies."

"Yes," Henchard replied, still not daring to look Newson in the eye. "If she had perceived it the right way, she would never have left

me. But one didn't expect that as she had no advantages at all except being able to write her own name."

"I had no intention of deceiving her," Newson explained. "I hoped she would be happy with me. But it seemed that tragedy followed her. Your child died and we had another. All was well. But then someone she had trusted with her history told her that I had no claim on her and our relationship was nothing but a farce. From that day on, she was not happy living with me. She declared that she must leave me and so when I went to sea again, I gave her the impression that I had died. My reason for doing this was only to give her happiness as I thought that if I feigned my death, she would return to you and our child would have a home again. I arrived only a month ago and learnt that Susan was dead but our child is still alive. Where is my Elizabeth-Jane?" he asked Henchard.

"She's dead too," Henchard lied. "Surely, you heard about it."

The sailor was shocked; aghast, he took a step back. "Elizabeth-Jane dead?" he exclaimed. "What use is my money then?"

"Where is she buried?" Newson demanded after a while.

"Right next to her mother," Henchard lied again.

"When did she die?"

"A little over a year ago."

"Alas!" Newson exclaimed. "My journey has amounted to nothing. I shall take your leave and not trouble you anymore," he said mournfully and left Henchard.

Henchard thought about what he had done, but the truth was that he had begun to depend upon Elizabeth-Jane and loved her like his own daughter. The thought of letting her go was inconceivable. But then, Newson would return if he came to know the truth. Henchard dressed quickly and exited his rooms to follow Newson. He had suspected nothing and had boarded the coach to leave Casterbridge.

The sailor had been simple enough to believe him and Henchard felt a sense of absolute shame. But he also started to panic, now that he had lied to keep Elizabeth-Jane away from her father. Henchard tried to calm himself down by walking to a place called Ten Hatches Hole that was situated at the east of Casterbridge. Moors and meadows were concentrated here through which plenty of water flowed. Henchard cast his eyes into the water and recoiled in shock. He had just seen his own dead body floating in the water!

For Henchard, who was very superstitious, this sight seemed like a supernatural vision. He walked home in a daze and saw Elizabeth-Jane waiting for him. She still called him 'Father'. Henchard requested her to accompany him to Ten Hatches Hole, but the body had disappeared.

"But, I clearly saw it," Henchard protested.

"The effigy!" Elizabeth-Jane exclaimed suddenly. "They must have thrown it into the

water at Blackwater out of fear of being caught by the magistrate's men. It must have flowed down from here," she concluded.

"But why did I see my image?" Henchard protested. "Where is the other effigy? Where's her image? They killed her with their act. Why am I still alive?"

Elizabeth-Jane was deeply saddened at his state and offered to live with him again and take care of him.

"But how can you forgive my cruelty towards you?" Henchard asked.

"I have forgotten it already," Elizabeth-Jane replied.

The next morning proved that Elizabeth-Jane had been correct in her assumption. Both the effigies were found far from each other in the same stream, but the figures were destroyed and the whole episode was hushed up.

Chapter Eighteen

Leaving Casterbridge

The fear that Newson would return and claim Elizabeth-Jane as his own haunted Henchard night and day. But Newson did not come back!

Elizabeth-Jane lived with Henchard and took care of him and a year went by. Henchard had opened a small retail seed and grain shop that had flourished over a year. Both Henchard and his step-daughter were happy and Elizabeth-Jane controlled the entire business. She also took long walks into the country twice or thrice a week, mostly towards Budmouth. Henchard spotted Farfrae staring at Elizabeth-Jane one day and was reminded that the Scotsman had

once had feelings for her. Henchard realised slowly that on her outings, Elizabeth-Jane spoke to Farfrae whenever the opportunity presented itself. The thought pervaded his mind with pain and jealousy.

"He intends to snatch her as well," Henchard exclaimed when he spotted the two one day. But Henchard realised that he had no right to interfere in their business.

"Let me leave everything to fate," Henchard concluded as he swore not to put any obstacles in their path. "If I am to be doomed by being parted from her, so be it!"

Unknown to Henchard, the meeting of Farfrae and Elizabeth-Jane were rather innocent, devoid of any romantic notions. But their meetings became more regular as the time progressed and one day Henchard's worst fears came true.

He spotted the two together and hid behind a wall near them.

He heard Farfrae address her as "My dearest, Elizabeth-Jane" and saw him kiss her while

Elizabeth-Jane quickly looked around to see if they had been spotted. Henchard slowly followed them back to Casterbridge, devastated by the knowledge that his only friend in the world would be separated from him now and would hate him too.

Soon, Casterbridge was filled with gossip about how the Mayor was often seen with the step-daughter of the bankrupt Henchard.

One day, Henchard was standing on the road when he saw a man at some distance walking towards town from Budmouth. Using his telescope, Henchard saw that the man was none other than Newson. Henchard dropped the telescope in shock and waited. But he could not see Elizabeth-Jane, something had caused her to abandon her plans to walk that day. He rushed home to discover her there.

"Father, I've received an anonymous letter from someone," she declared innocently. "The sender has asked me to meet him either at Budmouth road at noon or at Mr Farfrae's house in the evening. He claims that he had come to see me earlier but was tricked so he did not get to meet me. I do not comprehend this mystery, but somehow I feel that Donald is behind this. May I go?" she asked.

"Yes," Henchard replied with a heavy heart.

"I must tell you something, Elizabeth-Jane," he confessed. "I intend to leave Casterbridge."

"Leave Casterbridge?" she exclaimed. "Leave me?"

"You can manage this small shop by yourself now," Henchard said. "I'd rather go into the country and follow my own way in isolation and leave you to pursue your own goals and dreams."

Henchard now saw that Elizabeth-Jane was crying.

"I am sorry that you have decided this," she said with tears in her eyes. "I wanted to marry Mr Farfrae, but I did not realise that you did not approve of this match."

"I approve of anything that you desire, my love," Henchard said emotionally. "Even if I did

not approve it would be of no consequence. I want to go away. Besides, my presence might upset things in the future and it is best for all of us that I leave."

"You shall not attend my wedding then?" Elizabeth-Jane enquired.

"I do not wish to come," he said forcefully. "But think of me sometimes when you are happily married. You'll do that, won't you? Remember me when you are married to the richest and best man in town and don't hate me when you know about my sins. Remember that I have always loved you and that I always will."

"It must be because of Donald," she sobbed.

"I am not asking you to not marry him," Henchard replied. "But promise me that you will not forget me when he..." Henchard stopped. He wanted to ask her not to forget him when Newson arrived.

Elizabeth-Jane promised and Henchard left Casterbridge that very evening. No one but Elizabeth-Jane knew of his departure and

she escorted him till the second bridge on the highway.

When Elizabeth-Jane reached Farfrae's house, he announced dramatically, "He is waiting for you!" and led her to Richard Newson. It was an emotional reunion. After all, Elizabeth-Jane had grown up in Newson's care. Farfrae invited Captain Newson to be his guest and offered that his wedding with Elizabeth-Jane take place in his own house. Newson agreed heartily.

Elizabeth-Jane was shocked when Newson revealed that Henchard had told him that she was dead.

"I had promised never to forget him," she said. "But I think I should erase him from my memory forever."

Chapter Nineteen

A Father's Love

Henchard reached Weydon-Priors after a long and tiring journey of six days. He planned to do penance for his sins and then go to another part of the country. Here, Henchard found work as a hay-trusser. But he missed Elizabeth-Jane.

One day, he heard the name 'Casterbridge' from a wagon driver's mouth. He made some inquiries of the occupants in the wagon and found out that Mr Farfrae was to marry on Martin's Day.

Henchard wanted nothing more than a chance to see Elizabeth-Jane for one last time, to seek her forgiveness and give his blessings

and love. He left for Casterbridge, and two days before the event he bought some presentable clothes. Once satisfied that his appearance was respectable, he set about purchasing a gift for Elizabeth-Jane. Henchard was confused about what to buy her and lingered near the shop windows, walking up and down the street.

He arrived at Casterbridge to learn that Donald Farfrae and Elizabeth-Jane were now man and wife. Henchard reached Farfrae's residence where he could hear the sound of celebrations in full swing. But he could not muster the courage to enter the house. He did not want to invite her scorn and earn the displeasure of her husband and entered the house from the back, through the garden. He kept his present — a caged bird — under a bush to make his entry less awkward. The old lady who was the housekeeper spotted him and led him to the back-parlour. Then she went and informed Elizabeth-Jane.

"It is you, Mr Henchard," she said as she entered the room.

"Mr Henchard?" he recoiled. "Pray don't be so cold, Elizabeth-Jane."

"I would have always loved you," she said bitterly. "But you deceived me by telling me that my father was not my real father. You even told him I was dead to deceive him and broke his heart."

Henchard thought about explaining everything but then chose to remain silent.

"Don't worry because of me," he said instead. "I admit I have been wrong in coming to see you. Please forgive me! I shall never bother you again, Elizabeth-Jane. Goodnight and goodbye!"

Before Elizabeth-Jane could think of her next course of action, Henchard had exited the room and had disappeared.

Chapter Twenty

Henchard's Will

Newson left for Budmouth three days after the wedding.

Elizabeth-Jane discovered the birdcage with the dead body of a goldfinch inside. No one knew how it had come there. But it was obvious that the bird had starved to death. One of the maids informed her that the farmer who had arrived on the evening of the wedding had been carrying it. Elizabeth-Jane realised that it had been Henchard's gift for her and a sign of his repentance. She buried the bird in the garden and in her heart forgave the poor man.

Elizabeth-Jane told Donald everything and sought his help to find Henchard as she wanted to make peace with him. Farfrae did not object. He had no hatred in his heart for Henchard. But it was not an easy task to locate Henchard as he had become a changed man.

After a long and arduous search of several days, the couple abandoned their search. They were miles away from home now and decided to rest their horses in a village. They reached an elevated position as they travelled towards the village and spotted a man emerge from the foliage of the trees.

"Is that poor Whittle?" Elizabeth-Jane asked. It was indeed Abel Whittle, who was residing in a small cottage there.

"He was very kind to Mother when he was here," Whittle said sadly. "But he was rough to me as usual."

"Who?" Farfrae asked urgently.

"Why, Mr Henchard, Sir," Whittle said. "He just left half-an-hour ago."

"He's not dead?" Elizabeth-Jane asked, her voice full of anxiety.

"Yes ma'am, he is," Whittle replied sadly. "He left a piece of paper pinned to his bed. I can't read but I'll get it for you."

Whittle returned with a crumpled piece of paper. Written on it in pencil was,

Michael Henchard's Will

"Elizabeth-Jane Farfrae should not be informed about my death or be made to grieve for me. I should not be buried on ground that is consecrated. No one should be asked to toll the bell, nobody should witness my dead body, no mourners should walk behind on at my funeral, no flowers must be planted on my grave and no man, or woman must remember my name.

Michael Henchard"

"Oh! Donald!" Elizabeth-Jane exclaimed. "There is so much bitterness in his words. I can't bear it! I was so cruel to him when we parted. But we cannot change his will and everything must happen as he wished."

Though Elizabeth-Jane respected her stepfather's last wishes, she could not help wonder that she had been fortunate in her life because she had gotten so much more in life than she had deserved. There were many who were more deserving but received much less in comparison. She wondered at the unpredictability of the unforeseen. The man who had been bestowed with such tranquility had experienced only pain in his lifetime. Henchard's life seemed to epitomise that happiness and was nothing but an occasional episode in a general drama of pain.

About the Author

■ Thomas Hardy

Thomas Hardy was an English poet and novelist. He was born in the village of Upper Bockhampton in Dorset, England in 1840. His father was a stone mason as well as a violinist. His mother was an avid reader and thanks to his parents, Hardy was introduced to architecture and music and grew to love them. These interests were evident in his novels as well as the lifestyles of the country folk. So was his passion for all types of literature. Hardy taught himself Latin, German and French by reading the books he found in Dorchester, the nearby town.

At sixteen, Hardy was apprenticed to a local architect but would study in the evenings with Greek scholar Horace Moule. In 1862, Hardy was sent to London to work with the architect Arthur Blomfield. For five years, Hardy studied the cultural scene in London as well as classic literature. He chose to return to Dorchester and took with him the burning desire to write.

Hardy's most accomplished literary works include *The Mayor of Casterbridge*, *The Return of the Native*, and *Far from the Madding Crowd*. Thomas Hardy died in 1928 aged 87 after a long and highly successful life. But his legacy shall live on forever.

■ Characters

Michael Henchard: The novel's title, 'The Mayor of Casterbridge' is dedicated to Henchard, who is the protagonist. Henchard is twenty-one years old when the novel begins and sells off his wife to a sailor in a drunken rage at a country fair. Eighteen years later, Henchard rises to become the mayor and the biggest corn merchant in the town of Casterbridge. He tries to atone for his youthful crimes by giving up drinking but goes downhill in his career as he engages in a fierce business battle with a popular Scot named Donald Farfrae.

Susan Henchard: She is Michael Henchard's wife when the novel begins but becomes Newson's wife when Henchard sells her. She is a docile, unassuming woman who keeps Henchard's and Elizabeth-Jane's identities a secret to portray a picture of perfect family harmony.

Elizabeth-Jane Newson: The daughter of Susan and Newson, Elizabeth-Jane bears the same name as Susan and Henchard's child, who died shortly after Henchard sold Susan. As the novel progresses, Elizabeth-Jane transforms herself from an unrefined country girl into a cultured young lady and an independent woman. Though she experiences immense hardship, she maintains an even temperament throughout.

Donald Farfrae: He arrives in Casterbridge at the same time as Susan Henchard and Elizabeth-Jane. Farfrae's business skills, good humor, and charm make him very popular among Casterbridge's citizens. But he becomes Henchard's rival after he quits his employ. Henchard is partly responsible for Farfrae's estrangement from Elizabeth-Jane whom he loved but had to marry Lucetta. But Farfrae remains fair-minded, patient, and even kind to the bankrupt Henchard. He also succeeds him as mayor and is reunited with Elizabeth-Jane when the novel ends.

Lucetta Templeman : A woman whom Henchard meets, courts, and proposes to marry after Susan dies. Lucetta and Henchard were romantically involved before Susan arrived in Casterbridge and Henchard chose her over Lucetta. Lucetta employs Elizabeth-Jane when she expresses her desire to leave Henchard's house after her mother's death. Lucetta chooses Farfrae and marries him when she learns that Henchard had sold his first wife. Like Henchard, she is guided by her emotions, and her reactions are thus not always rational.

Newson : He is the sailor who is Elizabeth-Jane's father and the man who bought Susan from Henchard. Newson appears only in the beginning and the end of the novel and had faked his own death so that Susan and Elizabeth-Jane could live a happy life. Newson returns to claim Elizabeth-Jane and hurts Henchard unknowingly.

■ Questions

Chapter 1

- *What was so strange about the couple that walked together?*
- *How did the hay-trusser sell his wife to the sailor?*

Chapter 2

- *What was the oath that Henchard took?*
- *Where and why did he take such an oath?*

Chapter 3

- *Why did Susan Newson return to the fair?*
- *What message did the furmity woman give Susan?*

Chapter 4

- *Describe the conversation between Henchard and Donald Farfrae.*
- *How did Farfrae entertain the guests at the Three Mariners? Describe the effect he had on other people.*

Chapter 5
- *Where did Henchard meet Susan? Why did he choose the venue?*
- *What was the plan that Henchard shared with Susan?*

Chapter 6
- *What was the secret that Henchard shared with Farfrae?*
- *How did Henchard's business prosper under Farfrae's supervision?*

Chapter 7
- *Why was Abel Whittle always late for work?*
- *Why did Henchard and Farfrae argue over Whittle coming to work?*

Chapter 8
- *What were the contents of Lucetta's letter to Henchard?*
- *Why had Susan Henchard written anonymous letters to Elizabeth-Jane and Farfrae?*

Chapter 9
- *Why did Elizabeth-Jane agree to take Henchard's surname? Why had she refused to do so earlier?*
- *How did Henchard discover the contents of Susan's note and what did he learn? Describe in detail.*

Chapter 10
- *What was Miss Templeman's offer to Elizabeth-Jane? Why did she accept?*
- *What did Lucetta write to Henchard about?*

Chapter 11
- *Describe Pip's meeting with Estella.*
- *What happens between Estella and Mrs Havisham in Kent?*

Chapter 12
- *What did Henchard instruct Jopp about? Why?*
- *Why did Lucetta consent to marry Henchard against her wishes?*

Chapter 13
- *How did Henchard save Lucetta's life?*
- *Why did Elizabeth-Jane decide to leave Lucetta's house?*

Chapter 14
- *How did Henchard become bankrupt?*
- *What offer did Farfrae make to Henchard?*

Chapter 15
- *How and why did Henchard break his oath? Describe in detail.*
- *Why did Jopp want to take revenge against Lucetta?*

Chapter 16
- *How was Henchard humiliated before the Royal Personage?*
- *Describe Jopp's plan to take revenge against Henchard and Lucetta.*

Chapter 17
- *Why did Newson arrive to meet Henchard? Describe their conversation.*
- *Why did Henchard lie to Newson?*

Chapter 18
- *Why did Henchard decide to leave Casterbridge?*
- *What did Henchard ask Elizabeth-Jane to promise?*

Chapter 19
- *What gift did Henchard purchase for Elizabeth-Jane? Why did it not reach her?*
- *Describe the conversation between Elizabeth-Jane and Henchard.*

Chapter 20
- *What news did Abel Whittle have for Elizabeth-Jane and Farfrae?*
- *What did Henchard's will state?*